AWFUL ANNIE STORIES

When Aunt Binkie comes to stay she drives the family mad, droning on all the time about 'the Good Old Days' and Perfect Percy, her late husband. But, surprisingly, Annie becomes her closest ally ... and all because of a small stray Yorkshire Terrier called Percy. And soon Binkie decides she really must go home!

Annie has trouble with maths, so her teacher lends her an extraordinary machine called Nippy Numbers for a week – but Annie forgets it and it gets mixed up with a load of old jumble! In her desperate attempts to recover it she rescues fishy Mr Smurthwaite from burglars, discovers Mr Peggs's stolen car and amazes her mother and sister with her adventures.

Although Awful Annie isn't often in her parents' good books, here are two stories which show that she can come out on top in spite of everything.

J. B. Simpson has lived in or near Oxford for thirty years. She now runs a village inn near Wantage, and as well as writing she teaches in Sunday School. Jean Simpson also gives talks and lectures on puppetry, is interested in all aspects of Punch and Judy and gives shows at Covent Garden, the seaside and elsewhere.

AWFUL ANNIE STORIES

J. B. SIMPSON

Illustrated by John Lawrence

PUFFIN BOOKS

PUFFIN BOOKS

Published by the Penguin Group
27 Wrights Lane, London W8 5TZ, England
Viking Penguin Inc., 40 West 23rd Street, New York, New York 10010, USA
Penguin Books Australia Ltd, Ringwood, Victoria, Australia
Penguin Books Canada Ltd, 2801 John Street, Markham, Ontario, Canada L3R 1B4
Penguin Books (NZ) Ltd, 182–190 Wairau Road, Auckland 10, New Zealand

Penguin Books Ltd, Registered Offices: Harmondsworth, Middlesex, England

Awful Annie and Perfect Percy first published by Julia MacRae Books, 1986
Awful Annie and Nippy Numbers first published by Julia MacRae Books 1987
Published in one volume in Puffin Books 1988
1 3 5 7 9 10 8 6 4 2

Printed and bound in Great Britain by
Cox & Wyman Ltd, Reading

AWFUL ANNIE
and
PERFECT PERCY

To Annie Farrer –
a perfect friend

Contents

1 Trouble in Store

Isn't it annoying when people make you wear clothes you don't like? "Oh, that *does* suit you, Annie," they say, standing back all smiles! Really, you know that what you've put on is ugly and babyish, and everybody at school will laugh at it. But what can you do?

I like old clothes best. Things you can do whatever you like in. Except for parties, of course. But then you have to be in the swim. You can't make the same dress last and last. Best I like the fancy ones you see on bigger girls. Worst I like the ones people make for you, so you have to stand about trying them on.

So when my mother's old Aunt Binkie turned up on one of her long visits saying, "I am going to make you a frock, Annie," my heart sank. She made one for my older sister Carole once. It lasted *five years*! Carole hated this dress. She thought it was dingy. I thought so, too. Every time Aunt Binkie came, she let it out or took it down. So one day Carole stood too near the fire in it, and the dress got scorched. Carole pretended this was an accident, but I could tell Aunt Binkie knew otherwise.

"What sort of a dress would *you* like, Annie?" she enquired, last time she arrived. Out came the tape measure and the paper and pencil. "Now stand still, do! Don't hold your tummy in while

I measure you! My goodness, aren't you fat?"

I begged my mum not to force me to have this dress made. But it was to no avail. Making dresses

kept her quiet, said my mother. It's true Aunt Binkie does a lot of talking. Always about one of two things. Either 'The Good Old Days', when things were so much better all round, or Perfect Percy, her late husband.

The way she kept on and on about Uncle Percy made our dad grit his teeth. "Did old Percy wear wings while still on earth?" he used to groan. I think he thought Aunt Binkie was getting at him – suggesting that he wasn't up to her late husband's standard. But I found just the opposite. The way she went on about him made me almost hate Uncle Percy for having been so superior.

Aunt Binkie said she and I would go into
Kiddister together, and choose a pattern and some
material. It was winter-time, so we put on our
coats and hats, and took the afternoon bus.

Mind, a trip to the big shops always raised my
spirits. We've only got the one shop in
Pennymarsh, except for Mr Mungo's, half a mile
down the other way. Kiddister is eight miles to
the south. As the bus barged round the wintry
roads, I considered the matter which always rears
its ugly head foremost in a shopper's mind: *What
about cash?*

I hadn't got any. It was simple as that. Plainly Aunt Binkie had – but would she want to part with any? It seemed to me that now would be the time, rather than when she said goodbye. Could I persuade her to see the reason of this? All smiles and hope, I put the matter to her. Mentioning a *loan*, mind. I didn't want to seem greedy.

"I was thinking, Aunt Binkie, about money. Money is such a nuisance, isn't it?"

But she didn't seem to hear. So I looked out of the window, and she talked about Uncle Percy. They had loved shopping together, she said, she and Percy! She could see him now, trotting behind her with all the parcels, a sweet smile on his face. He was a saint.

11

"Gosh," I said – knowing now that Uncle Percy *was* a saint – "My dad hates shopping. My mum has to do it all herself."

Aunt Binkie sniffed. If Dad didn't like her, she didn't like him either. "Your father is utterly different," she said. "One of those big, belligerent men. Percy was tiny, but perfectly formed."

"Not a dwarf?"

"Oh, Annie, don't be silly, dear! Of course not. Just a small man with small bones." She sighed. "Always a smile for everybody," she said, "out of those tender brown eyes of his."

I didn't know what 'belligerent' meant, but I

could see that Dad and Uncle Percy were not in the same league. My father's smiles were not sent out to all and sundry. Nor could I see him trotting about carrying parcels. "I hope there are men like Uncle Percy about when I grow up," I said. "I'll marry one, and we will spend all our lives shopping."

Aunt Binkie sighed. Then she began to sniff. Next she took out a handkerchief, and dabbed at her eyes. She must have been thinking about Uncle Percy and all the fun they had together.

"I expect you have lots of happy memories, Aunt Binkie. I expect you sit by the fire and remember the good old days, when Uncle Percy smiled at everybody, and carried your parcels for you." As the bus rattled along, I tried to cheer her up. But it didn't work. What had seemed quite a nice, homely picture to me, was just a sad one for her. So I suggested she bought a budgerigar.

"My friend Cynthia's mother has got one. It keeps her company while Cynthia's at school. It can even talk! It says, 'Good Heavens, what's burning?', and 'Pretty Cynthia'. Cynthia isn't really pretty, but I bet she likes being told she is."

13

Aunt Binkie turned round, drawing in a great breath. For a minute I thought she had lost her temper. She can be quite batey when she chooses.

"Oh Annie, you are only a little girl, dear! You don't know what it is like to lose the one you love! To come downstairs in the morning and find the kitchen empty. To sit down opposite an empty chair."

Out came the handkerchief again, and it was quite a relief when the bus stopped sharply, then flew down the hill and rounded the corner into Kiddister.

"We won't go trudging round the town," she said, as we climbed out, "we will go straight to Sherlock and Young, and see what they have there."

But although she looked at everything they had, nothing at Sherlocks seemed to please her. What a relief! Then I had a good idea. "Let's go up to Women's Wear, on the first floor, and buy something nice for you instead."

But lo and behold, she didn't like the things in Women's Wear either. She said they were shoddy, baggy, flimsy, tatty, and badly finished off. Such ugly colours, too! Clothes were not the things of beauty they had been when *she* was young.

A lady of her age who was trying on a coat said, "I beg your pardon, but I quite agree with you!" The two struck up a friendly conversation.

Seeing me standing there yawning, Aunt Binkie asked, "Now, Annie, why don't you go and look at the toys down in the basement? Come back here in ten minutes' time."

2 The Two Smugglers

All the best stuff at Sherlocks is down in the
basement. The things I like, that is. Not just the
toys – though there is a huge selection of those.
Such pretty colours everywhere, cups and plates
with flowers painted all over them, fancy bags
and baskets. Then, the joke animals! Those
lifelike snakes, and as for the spiders, they fairly
make me rush past! There are some big black
spiders about now, called Miss Muffet Spiders.
They fly along the floor when you wind them.
Barry Bates brought one to school once, and it
scuttled over the mat just when Mrs Peggs was
taking some important visitor round. She let out a
scream, and Mrs Peggs picked it up, and put it in
her pocket, and it kept on buzzing and whizzing

16

and wouldn't stop. Barry went crimson, laughing, but I could tell from the look Mrs Peggs gave him that he wouldn't laugh much when she came back and told him what she thought of him.

Today, I looked at some comical mugs, with frogs stuck just on the inside. When you drank, the liquid went through the frog first, before coming to your mouth. I looked at these until a lady shouted, "Don't touch those, please!" Then I made my way through to the Pets Department.

"Why the Pets Department?" you ask. Because

of my dream. My dream about having my own dog. My father is always kind when I ask about my dog. But he says feeding a dog and keeping it going comes very expensive.

"You can't economise on a dog," he says. "You've got to give it the best there is going. In time, Annie, in time. When I'm a rich man."

Meanwhile, I gazed at what they had in the department. The price of the best dog bowl! I said to myself, "It ought to be made of gold, not plastic!" I was just getting almost as worked up as Aunt Binkie herself, when out from among the bowls and baskets crept a little brown dog.

It was a furry little figure, almost silky its coat was; it wagged its tail pathetically and licked my hand. I could see it was looking for a friend, and had decided I was a person who it might trust.

"That's been here all day," said the shop woman. "Nobody knows whose it is." She stood there, her arms folded across her front and looked down at the little dog from her big height. "Maybe someone wanted to get rid of him," she went on. "People buy dogs, then they can't afford to feed them. Pity, he looks quite a well-bred dog.

He's a Yorkshire Terrier. I've given him some
water. Well, I shall let him roam till this evening,
then ring the police.''

"That dog hasn't just been here today," said
another woman, crossing the floor, "he was here
yesterday, and the day before. He must creep into
the store rooms at night, poor little thing.
Nobody's asked after him. Well, the police will
keep him for a few days and then if they can't
find out whose he is, they'll shoot him.''

"Oh, not shoot him surely, how barbarous!" cried the other lady. The tiny little dog stood there snuffling, his tail between his legs, while the two women discussed different methods of bumping him off.

An old gentleman who was choosing a lead turned round with a smile and gave the little dog a pat. "What's *your* name?" he asked.

"He's called Percy," I said. The name just flew out of my lips.

"*Percy*?" repeated the first shop assistant. "Do you know this little dog?"

"Oh yes," I said. "The lady who he belongs to is up in the Dress Department."

"You'd better collar him, then," she said, "and take him to her. And tell her to take better care of him in future."

I collared him. He was a dear little shining dog, not much bigger than a rat. "There there, Percy," I said, "come upstairs, now!" He snuggled down in my arms. Before I went off upstairs, I stopped at the sweet counter on the ground floor. Yummy! Sherlocks sell chocolates like you never see anywhere else.

Then I went up to the next floor. Aunt Binkie was still talking to her new friend. She was boasting about the smart weddings she had dressed, in her day. "Oh yes, I made all the robes

for Lady Bombazine's daughter," she was saying.
"The bridesmaids had deep blue velvet dresses,
with tight bodices and gathered skirts, and the
bride's dress had such gigantic sleeves! It took me
two days and nights, sewing all the tiny buttons
on the cuffs." She swung round and saw me.

"Annie!" she gasped. "You've bought a little
dog!"

"Oh how sweet," cried her new friend. "Oh,
what a little darling. Oh, I do like your little dog."

Well, God is good, as Henry Rennie's granny
says. God is love. What with this lady loving this
scrap of a dog, and stroking it, and the dog licking
her hands, and Aunt Binkie being so surprised, I
managed to tell them both the truth.

Now I can't always do that. Good inventions
jump into my mind, and queue up, ready to burst
out when needed. *Lies*, my sister Carole calls
them. I suppose that's what they are. Like
suddenly pretending I knew this little dog, and
his name was Percy.

Once I got back to telling the facts, I could
breathe more deeply. The two old ladies were
sympathetic, too.

"How dreadful!" they cried, when I explained that in a few days' time, Percy might meet his doom.

"Sometimes the police shoot them, if they're strays; or scientists stick needles into them – oh, poor little Percy, what will be your fate?" I moaned, burying my face in his fur.

"Percy?" repeated Aunt Binkie in amazement. "Is that his name?"

"What an unusual name for a dog!" exclaimed her new friend. "I do like that name – Percy. Why, it seems to suit him."

Aunt Binkie was very pleased when I suggested we took Percy back in the bus. But what would my father say, she kept asking? Nothing very nice was the answer, both of us decided. But we took him just the same.

Here's what was so comical – all the bus journey into Kiddister Aunt Binkie had droned on about the *old* Percy, how saintly he was, how helpful and so on. All the bus journey back from Kiddister, she sat there doting on the *new* Percy. The one which sat on her lap, and gazed up at her adoringly.

I noticed she seemed a whole lot nicer with Dog Percy on her lap. He seemed to bind us together. As the bus sailed round the country lanes, we were quite a happy trio, Aunt Binkie, Percy and I.

We got to Pennymarsh just before the shop shut, so Aunt Binkie asked me to go and buy Percy a tin of dog food. Then the three of us made our way home in the dark.

3 The Secret Guest

My older sister Carole *did* look pretty. She was wearing a bluish-greenish dress, which stuck out all round her, and she had a pierrot's cap which fitted over her hair. Our mum stood in front of the fire, arranging each little curl, so that it fitted neatly with the others under the cap. Carole's eyes were made up with big black lashes, her cheeks were bright red, and really you might have thought she was grown-up. Yet in spite of all this prettiness, and a lovely smell of perfume, she was in a really bad mood and grumbling like mad.

She was going off to a disco with Mike Bates.

She kept pretending it was because he was late that she was angry. "Trust wretched Mike to let me down!" She nodded to Aunt Binkie, who

admired her dress, but she hadn't a word to say to me.

"Fancy you going about with Mike Bates," I said, to make her crosser still. "He's ugly, he's silly, and he's Barry's brother."

"I must say I never liked him either," said our mum through a mouthful of hairpins.

We didn't make Carole any happier. She said that if Mike didn't show up soon, she was going to the dance on her own. She'd only agreed to go with Mike, so as to make her real boyfriend, Bob Bright, suffer. Bob had been acting so hard-to-talk-to lately, she wanted to teach him a lesson.

26

"Carole made that dress herself," I told Aunt Binkie, who was getting rather left out of all this. Aunt Binkie said what a lovely dress, a pity she had chosen nylon though, and didn't it dip rather at the back? Should she stand so near the fire, what if it went up in flames? They both shot dark looks at each other. Then Aunt Binkie caught my eye, and sort of winked, and I knew we were both thinking about Percy.

The little dog Percy, that is, not her late husband.

I tell you what I'd done with Percy. I'd put him in our garden shed. First I gave him all the dog food, which he ate greedily, then I poured him out a bowl of water. He seemed quite happy in his new headquarters, and when I peeped in through the window, I saw him lying fast asleep on a sack of bulbs.

I knew our dad wouldn't be home till late, so he wouldn't find him. Carole was too taken up with herself and her dress to take an interest in anything else. Best of all, our mum thought that she'd walk with Carole down to the village hall where the dance was being held. She wanted to talk to somebody there.

"But what about you two? Are you going to start on Annie's dress this evening, Binkie? You haven't shown us the material, yet."

Oh no, said Aunt Binkie, the material at Sherlocks was much too shoddy. She would have to wait until she got home to find the right thing. But she and I would be perfectly happy on our own, we had plenty to talk about.

My mother looked surprised. People don't talk so nicely about me as a rule. Grown-up people don't always like me, funny, isn't it?

"I hope you aren't up to anything, Annie?" she said. "Now if Mike Bates calls, tell him Carole and I are on our way down to the hall."

Off they went, arm in arm.

"Phew!" I said, fanning myself with the *Radio Times*. "Now we can think about Percy."

28

"The little darling," said Aunt Binkie, "where is he?"

I held up one hand, bidding her wait – then hurried out into the dark, and down to the garden

shed. Next moment Dog Percy, having flung himself into the house, was seated on her lap and licking her face, as if he'd known her all his life. You'd have thought she was his favourite person ever.

I considered Aunt Binkie as she sat all smiles in the lamplight. I couldn't help thinking that here was the answer to her problems. All that coming downstairs and finding her kitchen empty would be over if Dog Percy moved in. He could sit in the other chair, just where Uncle Percy once sat. He couldn't carry the shopping, true; but even dogs have their limits.

But could she keep him? What if the person who he had belonged to before suddenly wanted him again? Mind, the ladies working at Sherlocks had said he was going to be handed over to the police this evening.

"What ought we to do next, Aunt Binkie? We can't keep him secret for ever, can we?"

"Oh Annie, I just don't know, dear!" said she, smiling fondly on her little friend, and making doggy noises.

A brain-wave hit me. "I could go and ask Mr Foley! He might know what we could do. He's our vet, and he lives in Pennymarsh. He is always good in an emergency."

She seemed quite pleased with my idea. It was very sensible, she said. "Off you go, dear, I shall be happy as a lark till you come back."

"Don't open the door to any strangers, mind!"
This was only my joke. Yet I swear, as I said it,
there came a little silent warning in my ear. I can't
describe it, but I do remember it was there, after
I'd said, "Now don't go opening the door to any
strangers!"

4 The Awful Visitor

It was a very dark night, but that didn't matter.
I'm never afraid of the dark when I'm outside;
there are houses all round us, and I know
everybody in the village. I like to hear the owls,
and imagine the trees full of birds asleep. I used to
worry about them falling off the branches, but
Mr Foley told me they cling ever so tight. Once I
heard one tweeting in a great tall bush, and I went
near, and put out my hand, and they all started
singing at once. I like to think they were singing
hosannas, like angels, but perhaps they weren't!
Perhaps they were saying, "Look out, look out"
to one another or, "Be quiet all of you, you've
woken me up!" You never know with birds.

I didn't mind most of the darkness, but I admit

Mr Foley's drive seemed uncanny. It is long and winding, and there's no light there at all. Big fir trees on either side make it quite black. Worse, the tall lady who helps him was in a terribly bad mood, and didn't even want to hear my story.

"How dare you come bothering the poor man at all hours! Wait until surgery, Annie Ironside,

like everybody else has to!" she shouted, banging the front door in my face. A great big piece of plaster which must have been over the door fell down, and hit me quite hard.

I can't think why Mr Foley employs such a bad-tempered woman. She must be awful company round the place. If I was a bit older, I'd ask him to have me to help instead.

I went back to the road, wishing I could see a little better. Ours isn't a busy village as a rule, but it was Friday night. Cars with great dazzling headlights went roaring past. I was just pulling into the inside of the road, when whose face should I see, lit up brightly by headlamps, but our mum's! She had just come from the village hall with Cynthia's mother.

"Annie! Whatever are you doing out here on your own?"

I hardly knew what to say. What with the plaster hitting me, and Mr Foley's assistant shouting at me, I couldn't seem to muster a good invention.

"I came on an errand of mercy, Mum."

"An errand of mercy? Whatever are you talking about?" The music in the village hall was so loud that she had to shout to make me hear. I waved my arms about, showing I couldn't hear her either, but she is a very determined woman and seized my arm, saying I had no right to be wandering about in the dark. In the end I thought I'd better tell her about Percy. Perhaps when she saw the sweet scene – Aunt Binkie all smiles, Percy number two seated on her lap – she would understand.

"Well you see," I explained, "there was this little dog at Sherlocks."

"Don't say Aunt Binkie went and bought you a dog!"

"Good gracious no, Mum! It was just that here was this pathetic little thing. It was lost, and Aunt

35

Binkie, well she got sentimental over it, you see.''

"Come to the point, Annie. Explain what you're doing wandering out in the dark on your own. And hurry up, do, pick your feet up – whatever is all that din?''

She stopped, peering into the dark. There aren't any lamps in Pennymarsh. That means we don't pay high rates, but it also means we all go about falling on our noses. We three couldn't see much, but it did seem as if there was a lot of noise going on.

We started hurrying to catch up with it, and soon found that we were right at our own garden gate. Our front door was wide open, the garden was full of neighbours, and Dog Percy was racing wildly to and fro, barking shrilly.

My mother and Cynthia's fairly flew into the house. They pushed past several people who were going in and out. Aunt Binkie was stretched out on the sofa by the fire. A blanket had been thrown over her, and Mr Entwhistle, our next door neighbour, was putting what looked like a glass of whisky to her lips. Little Percy appeared from nowhere, and leapt up on her, and I was

36

thankful to see her hand stretch out and give him a limp pat.

"It's OK, Mum, she's not dead!" I shouted.

"Dead? I should think not!"

Finding Mrs Entwhistle there, as well as Mr Entwhistle, my mother begged them to tell her whatever was happening.

"Your dear aunt has had a great shock," hissed
Mr Entwhistle. "We are trying to calm her
down." He bustled round gingerly, as if our house
was a hospital.

"A shock? What sort of a shock?" demanded
my mother.

"She will tell you herself, when she feels a little
better." Mr Entwhistle kept cautious eyes on
Aunt Binkie, as if she might go up in smoke at
any moment. Mrs Entwhistle took her pulse.

"Do you know anything about all this, Annie?"

"No, Mum!"

"Somebody had better tell me," she groaned,
and sitting down near her aunt, she said, "There

there, Bink, what's all this about?"

"His face," crooned Aunt Binkie, shuddering, but not opening her eyes.

"*Whose* face?"

"Ah! Whose face!" Mrs Entwhistle nodded. "That is what we asked ourselves."

"We only saw his back view," said Mr Entwhistle, "but that was bad enough." He tried out some new methods with Aunt Binkie. He knelt down and said, "We shall soon feel much, much better." He took out a neatly-folded handkerchief, unfolded it, and waved it about in front of her face.

Mr Entwhistle drives a St John's Ambulance. He goes to fêtes and shows with it. Just when you hope you are having a really good time, you see him with his ambulance back door open, messing about with stretchers.

"I am afraid we are up against a criminal this time," he said.

"One of those nut-cases you read about in the paper, I expect!" Mrs Entwhistle seemed thrilled to bits. There is nothing she likes better than a bit of trouble. When our dad got in a motor accident, and was brought home on a stretcher, there she was first, pounding on our door. The ambulance men had to ask her to get out of the way, so they could bring poor Dad indoors.

Another time, our cat got stuck up a tree. The first we knew about it was seeing Mrs Entwhistle hurling boots and shoes into the branches.

She must sit at her window, watching for things to happen all day long. No wonder *she* was the one who heard Aunt Binkie scream, and Percy yap, and was outside in time to see the dreadful man running for his life!

"Try to tell me about it, Binkie," begged my

mother, stroking Aunt Binkie's hand. But it was Dog Percy growling suddenly that revived the patient.

"Percy! Oh, you darling! Who was it saved my life? Who drove the horrid man away?"

"What horrid man?" shouted my mother, "and wherever did this dog come from? Is his name really Percy?" She exchanged looks with Cynthia's mother, who threw her eyes to the ceiling.

41

Then Aunt Binkie sat up a little, and began
slowly in a trembling voice to describe her
adventure.

"You see, Kathleen, while little Annie was out,
there came a knock at the front door. I went to
answer it, and when I opened the door, there
stood a man, the most evil-looking person I ever
saw in my life! He didn't even look like a man.
He looked more like an evil spirit from another
world."

My mother stared at her aghast. So did
Cynthia's mother. "Green," added Aunt Binkie,
"his face was green."

We all fell silent. Hoping he wasn't anywhere near. Trying to picture him. Or trying not to, in my case.

I felt so guilty, too. Fancy leaving her on her own! What if she had died of fright? Would I have been taken to court?

"Hello, hello, what's all this!"

My mother, who had leapt into the air when the front door rattled, flung herself onto my father in great relief, "Oh Harold! Thank goodness you're here!"

So now he had to hear the tale as well. It was jolly horrible, and I must say, if Dog Percy hadn't been uppermost in my mind, I should have been a shivering jelly.

"Describe the face again, Bink!" begged my mother.

"The face!" Aunt Binkie fixed her eyes on the drawn curtains. "It was the most dreadful face I

ever saw! So cruel! It suggested an ill-spent life, a wicked life. Full sneering lips, gathered up over

44

long sharp teeth – drawn brows – a frightful frown – ''

"Real life?" our dad demanded. "You didn't fall asleep watching telly?"

"No, no, the Entwhistles saw it, too, Harold!" our mum told him. "They said they actually saw the man run across the lawn!"

Just then Carole strolled in, dressed up in all her finery. "What's all this? A family get-together? I say, whose is this funny little dog?"

So *she* had to hear the story, too.

5 A Message in the Post

I must say, it got better every time, if you know what I mean by better. Aunt Binkie wasn't sure the man didn't wave a knife at her, and let out a sort of howl. As well as being so wicked-looking, he had hands with great big claws.

I saw a rather funny look cross our Carole's face. Ho-ho, I thought, what does my sister know? Why did she look like that, I wonder?

By now, Dog Percy had become the centre of attraction.

What sort of dog was he, everybody wanted to know? My mother said he was a dachshund. She'd known a dachshund once which could swim half-a-mile. Carole didn't think he was a dachshund. She thought he was a mongrel.

"Indeed he isn't!" cried Aunt Binkie angrily.
The very idea seemed to liven her up no end. "He
has the head of a very well-bred dog."

"Funny it getting lost in Sherlocks," said
Carole, "you'd think some fussy old woman
would keep an eye on her dog, wouldn't you?
Not turn her back on it, while she was spending
all her money."

"And what makes you think he belonged to a
fussy old woman?" Aunt Binkie wanted to know.
It's always the same with those two, they really

manage to put each other's backs up.

"I think he ran into Sherlocks from somewhere else," I said, "and then it was sort of cosy in there, so he stayed. I've often thought I'd like to spend a night in Sherlocks, as long as the electricity worked. Then I could walk round and round all the floors all night till I was quite worn out; then I could select a lovely bed in the Furnishing Department and go to sleep."

"Well, I think he's a sweet little chap," said my mother, taking him up in her arms.

My father had gone out to his shed, I think he wanted to get away from Aunt Binkie and her green-faced monster. He hadn't really taken in the arrival of Dog Percy. When he came indoors again, Dog Percy began barking shrilly, and made for his ankles. My father was furious. "What about this dog! Did he arrive with the mad visitor, or what?"

Aunt Binkie threw me a knowing smile. "You'd better ask little Annie," she said.

So I told him how Percy was lost, and how I'd found him prowling round Sherlocks, and how he might have been shot.

Dad shrugged his shoulders. "Oh well, I'd better ring up the police tomorrow I suppose," he said. "It's much too late to go bothering them about dogs at this hour. What a time you've all had! Good night, Mr Entwhistle. Good night, Mrs Entwhistle."

"My evening wasn't much better," grumbled my sister. "Mike Bates was late, and we had a quarrel. The music packed up, and somebody trod all over my sandals, so I came home early."

"Off to bed, the lot of you! That funny-looking dog can sleep in the shed." My father threw Percy a biscuit.

"Not unless I sleep there, too!" Aunt Binkie's outcry gave him a start. I daresay he would have been happy for her to sleep in the shed. But in the end he was forced to agree to Percy sleeping in her bedroom.

"I'll put a rug on the floor," said my mother. "Let him out if he whines, won't you?"

"Oh, I don't expect I shall sleep," she said, "not after all I've been through. No thank you,

Kathleen – I don't want a cup of cocoa, it would take more than *that* to calm me down."

She fairly shot upstairs, precious Percy under her arm.

The police were quite nice. They said as long as we gave them our names and addresses, we could hold on to the dog for the time being, and probably for ever.

"I'm not giving them ours," said my father, "that thing can't stay here."

51

"Give them *my* name!" ordered Aunt Binkie. "Mrs Barber, 5, Bingley Road, Riverstock." She turned to me, putting out her hands. "Annie, my dear! It was you who found darling Percy. Are you sure you trust me to look after him?"

Oh, said our dad, she didn't want him, she couldn't afford a dog. I nearly cried at these hard words. I did so want a dog of my own.

Mind, Percy wasn't altogether the dog of my dreams. He was too small, and yapped a great deal.

Then Aunt Binkie dropped a bombshell. She said it nearly broke her heart to have to say so, but she felt she ought to leave us straightaway. Otherwise Percy might settle down in our house and not want to go back to hers.

My father's face! Luckily he was standing behind Aunt Binkie, so she couldn't see it. It really lit up with joy. He never enjoyed Aunt Binkie's visits, what with her going on about the Old Days, and taking all our mum's attention.

However he gave a sigh, and shook his head, and said what a shame: "Still, Binkie, if that is your wish, then go you must."

We all waved goodbye to her next day. I gave Percy a parting kiss. Then Dad swung me up into the air and hugged me. "Good old Annie!" he said. "That little dog of yours got rid of Aunt Binkie double-quick! What would you like as a reward, eh?"

"A dog of my own," I said.

"A dog would eat us out of house and home," said Carole. "Besides, we can't spare the money. We're saving for that holiday abroad, not for a great pooch."

Our dad put his arm round me, saying he only wished he could afford a dog. He knew how much I'd always wanted one. He'd like one himself. Especially now that madmen seem to have taken to appearing in our garden!

I'd just given up all hope, when Aunt Binkie's letter arrived. My mother opened it, read it, then let out quite a gasp. "Just listen, you three!" We stopped eating toast and marmalade and put down our cups of tea.

"Dear Kathleen," recited our mum.

"Here is my usual thank you letter. My stay was short but happy, thanks to dear Annie . . ."

"Thanks to *who*?" jeered Carole, making silly faces.

"Dear little Dog Percy has settled down a treat," the letter continued, "we are the best of friends. Now when I saw her last, I promised to make Annie a dress. But since she is not a vain, self-centred girl like her older sister, I wonder if she would agree to another type of present? As she is a dog-lover like myself, I am sure she would. This is my plan. Each month, I will send

you by banker's order enough money to cover the upkeep for a dog *of her very own*. Meanwhile, enclosed is a small cheque to pay for a collar and lead and two bowls – and, of course, her *dog*."

The parents stared at each other. Carole made a rude remark under her breath.

"That settles that, then!" said our dad. "You shall have your dog, Annie, after all!"

"Digby," I said.

"What's that?"

"Digby. That's the name I'm going to call my dog."

"What an awful name!" jeered Carole. I could tell she was annoyed to hear herself called vain.

6 Carole's Version

That evening, after I'd gone to bed, Carole came
and sat down in my room. She wanted to know
how much money Aunt Binkie had sent me.

"Phew!" she exclaimed, when she heard.
"Mind, Annie, some of that ought to come to me."
"Why?"

"Well – it's a long story. If I tell you, do you
promise you won't go blabbing to your friend
Cynthia, and all that lot at school?"

"Promise."

"You won't tell Mum and Dad?"

"I won't say a word."

She hummed and hawed a bit. I could tell she
had something up her sleeve. Mind, I wasn't
going to part with any of Aunt Binkie's money in

a flash! Carole's jolly good at getting things she wants. She always keeps a good eye on anything which comes my way. Well, I don't mind yielding now and then, but this time the money was going to be for Digby.

"Tell me the story, then!" I sat up in bed, eager for news. It's nice when people come and talk to you, before you go to sleep. It just seems the right time for stories and secrets. Not that Carole is a restful sort of person. She's here, there and everywhere, picking things up and putting them down; 'a real fidgety Phil' my mother calls her.

She picked up my comb and began combing her hair. She has got such lovely long, silky hair, not

silly fuzzy stuff like me. Then she came over and
sat on my bed. She picked up my toy bear and
played with it. She undid its bow-tie and did it up
again.

"You remember that frightening man who

came and knocked on our front door and gave
old Aunt Binkie such a shock?"

"Don't make me shiver! I never saw him
myself. But I heard her describe him. Gosh,
Carole!" I stared at her in horror. "Don't say
you've seen him, too?"

Wearing a cool, faraway look on her face, she asked, "What if I have?"

"Carole! Weren't you scared stiff?"

"I was scared to death," she said, "I went hot and cold all over." But she didn't sound scared a bit. Then she put on a hideous face, lifted her shoulders high round her ears, and began creeping round the room on tiptoe, making her fingers into claws, and uttering blood-curdling noises.

"Carole! Stop!" Then all of a sudden, I saw she was joking. Old Carole can be quite a scream when she chooses. She is very good at imitations. Sometimes she comes in through the back door quietly, and calls out, "Coo-ee! Am I in the way?" in exactly the same way as Mrs Entwhistle likes to do. It always fools our mum and dad.

"You weren't scared of him, then, Carole?"

"Course not!" She stopped prancing about, and wearing her ordinary smile, she said, "I know who he was, that's why."

"You do? Who was he?" I nearly jumped out of bed.

"Mike Bates."

Having made this amazing announcement, Carole began to hum and sing, dancing round the room with my little bear as her partner.

"It couldn't have been! The Entwhistles would have known him!"

"It was. He came round to take me to the dance. Only I'd gone on ahead with Mum."

"But Carole, he's not that awful to look at! Aunt Binkie said the man had a green face. She said he looked as though he had led a wicked, ill-spent life!"

"Mike was wearing a mask. You know – one of those Frankenstein faces which fit over your own. They look horrible. And he'd got hold of two of those awful hands, with claws; haven't you seen them? He thought I'd come to the door, so I'd be the one to suffer. He hadn't reckoned on it being Binkie. I tell you, he was the one who was scared in the end! What with her yelling out, and the dog appearing from nowhere, and the Entwhistles

giving chase!"

We started to laugh. Carole laughed so much
she rolled about on the floor. I thought we'd
never be able to stop. When our mum came in,
she wanted to know what all the fun was about.
But we didn't tell her. Carole said goodnight to
me, and she even said "Happy dreams – about
your new *dog*, eh Annie?"

I lay and thought about it all. I thought about
Aunt Binkie and Percy, now settled down happily
in her house no doubt.

I thought about Mike Bates. Well, I ought to be grateful to him really. And to Carole. And to God. After all, God invented dogs.

"All good things around us
Are sent from Heaven above . . ."

My dog hadn't been sent yet. What sort would he be? Well, I could ask Mr Foley's advice. Maybe I could get a stray dog from a dogs' home.

I sighed. I'd never felt so happy before in all my life.

AWFUL ANNIE
and
NIPPY NUMBERS

To Jat –
a treasured husband

Contents

1 Mr Peggs can't be called careless

"Lay not up for yourselves treasures on earth,"
read out dear old Miss Tubb, the infant teacher,
"but lay up treasure in Heaven, where moth and
rust do not corrupt, nor do thieves break in
and steal."

What a pretty piece of the Bible, I thought!
It just fitted in with poor Mr Peggs and his car.
That was probably why Miss Tubb chose it.
She must know that moth and rust and thieves
apart, that smart car of Mr Peggs's is his chief
treasure.

Mr and Mrs Peggs live in a house attached to
Pennymarsh school. We children expect to see a
lot of Mrs Peggs, who is our Headmistress, and
very kind, but Mr Peggs is not like his wife

at all. He stands at his window and glares. He moans if we shout too loud. So when we see his yellow Rover swinging out of the gate we say, "Hooray, old Toothy's off!"

Mr Peggs takes terrible care of his car. He changes it each year, but always chooses a yellow one. "Worship the idol, worship the idol," my dad whispers, when he passes it.

Mr Peggs doesn't have a garage, so his car lives under a plastic dome. Or rather, it did, until the awful night when a thief came and drove it away.

"I thought I heard somebody," said Mrs
Peggs, when she told us all about it. "I sat up
in bed and said 'Hark!' My husband thought
I was dreaming. Till he heard the car start up.
Then he was out of bed in a flash — chasing up
the road in his dressing-gown — poor man!"

Nobody knew who had taken the car.
Nobody could find it. Every day, us children
would race into school calling, "Has it turned
up yet, Mrs Peggs?" Barry Bates boasted that
his policeman uncle would get his hands on the
thief in a flash. But his uncle didn't. Talk of
Mr Peggs and the missing yellow Rover kept
everyone happy for days.

Then lo and behold *my* treasure went missing,
too!

"Oh no, Annie!" you cry, "not dear old
Digby, your beloved dog?"

No! Not my best treasure. Indeed, not my
treasure at all. Treasure I'd been lent.

I'd better stop going on about poor Mr Peggs
and his missing Rover, and explain what this
treasure was which went missing in such a
hurry.

If you peep through the left-hand window of Pennymarsh School, at around about two-thirty on any Wednesday afternoon, you would see a small figure sitting at a low table. The eyes in the figure's head would be staring at a row of numbers, and the sort of noise you might hear coming from the figure's mouth would be "er –" or "um." Across the table from this small figure, seated in a large chair, you would see another, larger figure. That would belong to Mr Trencham, mathematical expert of the county. His noises would make more sense: something like, "Oh Annie – can't you *see*? Now, if ten equals X –"

Why should ten equal X? The window doesn't equal the chair! All right, all right – don't think I wouldn't like to understand – don't think I *want* to be so batty! Oh and I suffer, too. Most of all I suffer from these visits made by Mr Trencham every Wednesday, to give me extra maths coaching.

To think Mr Trencham drives round all the schools shedding misery and being paid! Not that he gets cross. No, he is ever so patient.

Beads of moisture stand out on his brow.
"Now look, Annie dear – for the fourth time –"
His pen wags up and down. He doesn't
scream. Nothing like that. But sometimes I can
almost think a scream is forming inside him.
"What I don't see, Mr Trencham, is what it
all relates to. I mean – if you showed me, well

hundreds of cakes, or flies, or leaves – but just numbers! Numbers of what? Now if you said you'd got a hundred hairs on your head for instance –"

"You flatter me, Annie," said Mr Trencham, mowing his thinning hair with one hand. It must be terrible for him really, seeing it all so clearly, and having to say everything again and again. There he is, living in a happy world of numbers, a-thousand-and-one-ing it along the country lanes in his car, and then he has to climb out and walk into the schoolroom and meet little nine-year-old ninnies like me who don't understand a word he says.

One day, Mr Trencham lent me what he called an Educational Toy. He opened the box, which was full of coloured knobs.

"Look on it as an aid, Annie," he said, "see it as your friend. See it as a blind man sees his stick." When I pointed out that a blind man couldn't see his stick, Mr Trencham said he only wished I could apply my sharp wits to mathematics.

"You will find this game most interesting,

Annie, I am sure. I will show you how it works.
You will find that when you do things the right
way, just see now," Mr Trenchham pulled some
of the knobs, "or should I say *listen* –" he
waited.

"WELL DONE!" said a crackly voice from
inside the box.

Mr Trencham laughed away, then put the
lid on the box, and said I might keep it for a
week, and take it home.

"It's called NIPPY NUMBERS," I said, reading it
off the top.

"What a name! Still, I suppose it's catchy. Now take care of it, won't you? The thing isn't mine." Off he went in his car, leaving this interesting gadget in my care.

Now I could see at a glance that NIPPY NUMBERS was expensive. I mean, it was all poshly got up together, and it had that voice, and everything. It was quite big, too – I had a job to carry it. You'd have supposed I would have been breathing NIPPY NUMBERS, NIPPY NUMBERS to myself reverently for a whole week, wouldn't you? Not a bit of it. In less than an hour, I'd forgotten its existence. I'd left it in the company of a lot of old hats and shoes, and gone home without it.

What happened was this. My friend, Cynthia, and I were making our way home from school, wondering how to make the most of a lovely summer evening, and me carrying NIPPY NUMBERS, when we noticed a sign saying JUMBLE, with an arrow pointing, stuck in a grassy bank.

"My mum's in the hall," explained Cynthia, "sorting stuff out, ready for the fête on

Saturday. She says they have got some lovely things this summer, Annie.''

''Let's go and have a recce, then, Cynthia!'' I pleaded.

There *were* some good things, too. Really nice long skirts and fluffy jerseys. Funny hats – we couldn't resist trying on those, and the fancy shoes, then prancing about giggling.

''Little girls always like wearing ladies' clothes,'' said old Mrs Renny, who was in the hall with Henry, her little grandson. He didn't

think much of Ladies Wear, why should he —
but his sharp eyes soon saw NIPPY NUMBERS.

"Let's have a look, Annie!"

"Well, you can have a go, Henry," said I in
lordly fashion, "providing you take great care
of it. It belongs to the county, you know, and
I have it on loan."

"I'll take care, I'll take care!" cried Henry,
his eyes shining. He jumped about like a
monkey, dragging the toy to a good position on
one of the tables. He's ever such an annoying
child, but he had a twin brother once, who got
run over, so people try to be kind to Henry to
make up. I must say, he was pretty quick with
NIPPY NUMBERS. The crackly voice said, "WELL
DONE" again and again.

"Wilt thou be my wedded husband?" asked
Cynthia. She had found a piece of net curtain,
and wound it round her head, like a bride.
I found all sorts of other pretty pieces among
the rummage. There were some plastic flowers,
which I gave her to carry. Then I found a huge
man's jacket and put it on, and we paraded
round the hall arm in arm, singing 'Love is the

sweetest thing'. Cynthia is mad on weddings, and if ever she has enough money to buy a record, it always has to be full of love and kisses.

"Bye-bye Annie, see you tomorrow."
"Bye-bye Cynthia, see you tomorrow."
I went home quite happy. I had tea, watched telly, and went to bed. Never a thought did I give to NIPPY NUMBERS. Then in the night I woke with a start.

Oh no! Mr Trencham's toy! What had I done with it?

My heart began beating fast. I remembered Mr Trencham's face, just before he lent me his costly toy. For a moment he had hesitated and looked doubtful, as if he wasn't sure if he should part with such a thing. Then he had pushed it across to me trustingly: "Take care of it, won't you, Annie? It isn't mine."

Take care of it! And what had I done? Carted it off to the Village Hall and put it down any old where, with a load of scarves and hats and dresses. Landed it among things which people deliberately gave away, because they didn't want them any more.

Worse, I had let Henry Renny play with it; Henry, who broke practically everything he picked up; who nobody with any sense would trust with a bar of soap.

I sat up in bed, clasping my knees. If it hadn't been dark, I should have rushed off to the Village Hall there and then.

My elder sister, Carole, has a favourite song she plays all the time; it's sung by a chap called Zack Washer, and it goes:

'No regrets, no regrets,
I'm never sorry, never worry,
Yah yah, keep yer moans,
Flesh is flesh and bones is bones –'

I hear her singing it round the house. It seems to suit her angle on life. But I'm not the same. When I think of the awful things I do, like losing Mr Trencham's toy, I want to scream.

Now Carole would know just what to do. I mean, she would know how to deal with Mr Trencham. I could picture her letting him know she'd lost NIPPY NUMBERS. First he'd ask:

"So how did you get on with the toy, Carole?"

"The toy, Mr Trencham?" She'd wear a

bright smile, and look at him as if she felt a little bit sorry for him. She'd pat her hair, and look vague and sigh.

"The Numbers game which I lent you."

"Oh, Mr Trencham! I can't tell you what a worrying time I've had with that game!"

"Oh? And how is that?"

"I do wonder if perhaps you ought to have lent it to me –" another sigh. Carole does wonderful sighs.

"How come?"

"Well, after school, I called in at the Village Hall, where I look at the old stuff they put out there for jumble. There's nothing much worth having as a rule, but I took a look at one or two things. Old Mrs Renny was in charge. She is a friend of ours, but she has this silly little grandson, Henry. You may know him? Well, Mr Trencham, it sounds perfectly stupid, but while my back was turned one or other of them just spirited it away."

"Spirited away NIPPY NUMBERS, Carole? You're joking!"

"I wish I *was*, Mr Trencham –"

And so it would go on. If it had been Carole who'd lost the wretched thing, that is.

But it wasn't Carole, that was the trouble. It was me.

2 Annie can

"What happened to my toy, Henry?"

"What toy, Annie?" He gazed up at me through his big pale eyes. I'd collared him in the school playground, and was holding hard on to his bony shoulders, so he didn't sneak away.

"The toy! The Numbers toy! The one I lent you in the Village Hall, when you were there yesterday with your granny!"

"I put it back, Annie, *leave go*."

"Back where?"

"You can't expect me to remember back where zackly. Back with the other stuff on the tables."

"What, with the jumble? But that's the stuff

to be sold, you great careless thing! Somebody
might buy it!"

"*Leave go* – course nobody won't buy it!
Nothing gets sold before Saturday! Speck your
silly old toy's safe! Pooh! I could do it all in
seconds. Mr Smurthwaite said, 'Oh that's for
infants', he said."

"Mr Smurthwaite? Who's he?"

"He's big fat Smurthy, cares for the horses
up at the Jet-Jettersons' house, he made your
toy say WELL DONE six times. Tell you what,
Annie – *leave go* – if it's bust, Mr Smurthwaite
bust it." Henry pulled himself free and shot
across the playground.

So after school, I got hold of Cynthia, and
dragged her down to the Hall. It was locked.
We looked through all the windows and saw
the piles of jumble still there on the trestle
tables. I couldn't see NIPPY NUMBERS. "Do you
think your mother would lend us the key,
Cynthia?"

But Cynthia's mother had gone into Kiddister,
and Cynthia said she wouldn't have the key,
anyway. Old Mr Dodds, who lives just behind
the Hall, would have it. Then we both shook
our heads, knowing that for anybody to get
anything out of mean old Mr Dodds, let alone
the key to the Village Hall, would be a miracle.

Cynthia went her way home, and I went
mine, dragging my feet along the road and
pulling straws out of the grassy bank. "Oh
Mr Trencham," I was saying in my mind, "er,
about your *toy* . . ." Then while I was busily
inventing all manner of excuses, I went through
our back door, and at once cheered up a little.
Four people were sitting round the table at
home – my mum and dad, Mrs Entwhistle (our
next door neighbour) and, Heaven be praised,

Henry's granny, who'd been handling all the
jumble. They were all drinking quantities and
quantities of tea, and eating chocolate biscuits,
and having a good laugh about Mr Peggs's
missing Rover.

"Of all the cars in Pennymarsh, the thieves
knew which one to choose! You wouldn't think
they'd look in a place like this village for a
four-wheeler, would you? But having done so,
they'd never find a better kept car than old
Toothy's. Surprised he doesn't sleep with it

under his pillow. I wonder where it is now?
Purring its way towards a re-spray, perhaps.
Well, well, there are some funny people about!''
My dad took a swig of tea, then started singing:

"Poor Toothy Peggs
He'll have to use his legs –"
"Sh, now Annie's here you're not to talk like
that!'' cried my mother. "So is there any news,
Annie dear? Did Mrs Peggs mention it at all?''
"Mention what?'' I was far away, still
thinking about NIPPY NUMBERS.
"The yellow Rover, dear,'' said my father.
"Poor old Toothy's car.'' He passed me the
chocolate biscuits, saying, "Can't you get it

back for him, Annie? You're a bit of a Sherlock Holmes."

"There are some funny people about these days, aren't there?" My mother shook her head.

"Talking of funny people," said old Mrs Renny, "what do you make of Mr Smurthwaite, Kathleen?"

"Mr Smurthwaite?" she said. "Fat, red-faced caretaker up at Benson House?"

"Comes from up north," added my father. "Drives a Mini pick-up."

"That's the man! Now do give me your advice. While I was up at the hall getting the jumble out, he took quite a fancy to a toy which was there. He and Henry had a game with it, and then he started asking me if he could buy it. Seems the little boy up at Benson House, the youngest Jet-Jetterson boy, is very backward with his sums. Mr Smurthwaite suggested he could give *him* the toy. It would be such a help to him, he said. Well – I told him we didn't usually let stuff go, until the sale itself. But he seemed so keen, and willing to pay, so I let him have it. Just thought I'd mention it. Course,

I put the money in the drawer.''

"What did Mr Smurthwaite do with it?"

They all four turned round, startled, and
stared at me. I had spoken in a sort of little
shout, quite alarming old Mrs Renny. It never
takes much to do that, living with Henry and
looking after him has reduced her nerves to
slivers. My mother asked whatever was the
matter with me, all of a sudden, and Dad said,
"Why the flashing eyes, little daughter? Did
you want that old Jumble Sale toy, to help you
with your sums?"

I didn't know what to reply. I simply didn't
dare confess the facts. What, and have them all

90

come down on me like a ton of bricks?

People don't always remember how hard it is, explaining at home what goes on at school, and at school, what goes on at home. If I'd said, "Well, as a matter of fact what you call an old Jumble Sale toy happens to belong to the County Educational Office," there would have been all sorts of fuss. Fuss from the parents, fuss from Henry's granny, and worst of all, one hundred per cent fuss from our neighbour, Mrs Entwhistle, whose nosiness always makes matters worse.

"Oh, I was just – interested," I shrugged and smiled. "I mean, fancy Mr What's-his-name buying it, that's all! Fancy him taking it off with him, as I expect he did."

"He paid for it with a generous hand," said old Mrs Renny, and repeated the fact that she had put the money in a drawer.

"Money for a toy like that!"

"Whatever's bitten you, Annie?"

"Oh nothing. I just wonder why he wanted it."

"I told you, dear, he wanted it for the little Jet-Jetterson boy, who it seems is very backward with his schooling." Then old Mrs Renny began wailing that she couldn't be expected to keep a watch over everything in this life, she only had one pair of eyes.

"Oh, you did perfectly right to get rid of it, dear," said my mother. "Nobody wants half of these old toys people keep bringing to Jumble Sales. Most of them have had so much wear and tear, they aren't worth anything." Then old Mrs Renny repeated that she only had one pair of eyes, and all agreed that it was a shame God hadn't given her another pair, what with Henry being 'everywhere at once'. Now they all began talking about Henry, Mrs Renny's favourite subject, and my least favourite, especially at the moment.

My mother glanced at me shrewdly. Again she asked whatever was the matter with me, going on like a cat on hot bricks: wouldn't I like to sit down?

"Oh no thanks – I'm just popping out – be back later. Bye-bye, everybody."

3 A shock for Mr Smurthwaite

Henry Renny sat on his garden wall, eating an orange.

"Henry," I said, "I've found out where NIPPY NUMBERS is. We'll go up to the big house straightaway and find Mr Smurthwaite."

"You can go," he said, "I'm not going."

"You've got to come with me, Henry. Tell you what, we'll call in at the shop and I'll get you an iced lolly. I've got a bit of money saved up. You've got to come, because I've never even met Mr Smurthwaite in my life."

Henry stumped along beside me sourly. I wonder what anybody would have made of the pair of us? I skipping round and round Henry, urging him on, and he such a scrap of a child,

94

grudging every step he took and looking more like a tiny man than a boy in those large trousers his granny makes him wear.

"You ought to look after your stuff better Annie! You know what Barry's uncle says. He says it's people's own fault, if they leave their stuff about and it gets nicked." Henry licked his raspberry lolly, moaning that he didn't see why he should have to be dragged into all this.

"All right, Henry, calm down –" Such a sweet yellow butterfly flew after us, I think it was after the iced lolly. As the two of us sped through Pennymarsh, Henry told me – as if I hadn't heard it already – that Mr Smurthwaite was a funny chap.

"In what way, funny?"

"He talks funny. And he's got a funny temper."

"Well, I hope he keeps his temper down to-day."

"I expect you do, Annie." Henry waved the butterfly away.

Just then, who should we see coming towards us but Mr Peggs. He is a tall man, pale without much hair. We don't often see him walking round the village, but what else could he do now without his yellow Rover?

We said hello to him, but he swung past looking bitter.

96

Henry made some rude remarks.

"I wish we could help him find his car," I said. "He must be jolly difficult to live with, pining for it all the time!"

"Spect his car is over the hills and far away," chortled Henry, "and who cares? I don't."

"Personally, I'd like to catch the chap who took it."

"You catch anybody! You're so slow you couldn't catch a snail!"

Henry was beginning to get on my nerves. I was just going to tell him so when a piece of his iced lolly fell off the stick, and he made such a scene, I decided not to upset him further. After all, he knew Mr Smurthwaite. I wasn't much looking forward to meeting the latter, after hearing what a funny temper he had. Best turn up with Henry, not risk a scene on my own.

"Here we are, then," said Henry, a moment or two later, "and don't forget it was *your* idea to go visiting him, not mine."

Benson House stands on the edge of the village. It is a huge place, and very old. The Jet-Jettersons aren't there much. They spend a lot

97

of time abroad. But their horses stay behind, and if the gate is open, you can glimpse their long, sweet faces peeping across the half doors of their stables.

We opened the big gate and went in, and we'd hardly gone a few yards when Henry said, "Look Annie, that's Mr Peggs's car!"

I gave a start. The last person I wanted to see was Mr Peggs. But then I saw that this wasn't his car at all.

"Don't be silly, Henry. That's a red car!"

"It's his car! It's his car a different colour. Look, see that bumper? See that gluey mark on the window, where Sally Anne went and stuck a row of stickers on it?"

"But it can't be!"

"I tell you it is."

I had a good look. To be truthful, I don't know anything much about cars. "But nobody would leave it in Pennymarsh, if they stole it —" I remembered my dad talking about funny people. And then I remembered old Mrs Renny saying, "Talking about funny people, what do you make of Mr Smurthwaite?"

"Perhaps Mr Smurthwaite pinched it!" I
whispered.

"Zackly! I was thinking zackly that!"

"And gave it a re-spray!"

"Zackly! I was thinking zackly that!"

The two of us proceeded a little further.

I'd never been right close up to this big

99

house before, and when I saw the great gardens, full of enormous lovely flowers, and the rosy brick walls, and all the stillness there was there, everything so beautifully planted, and the evening sun shining, I thought I'd like to keep walking round the place for ever.

"Smart," Henry breathed in my ear. "Shall we go away, Annie?"

"No, I'll ring the bell." I did. It was the sort
you pulled. It went *'clang-clang-clang'*, and I'd
hardly rung it before I wanted to hide. Henry
did hide. "Come out, Feebleness," I ordered,
dragging him back on to the doorstep.

I rang the bell again. It sounded loud enough
to bring all England to the door. Nobody came.

"Maybe Mr Smurthwaite lives round the
back," suggested Henry. It was his first good
idea. About now he started being sensible.

We went round the back. Everything looked
locked up. Then Henry found a door which
opened. He said we could creep in, and call

101

Mr Smurthwaite's name. So we did.

There were lots of kitcheny rooms at the back, and then we opened a door, and came into the proper part, and into all the great big smart rooms, with pictures hanging up and luscious furniture.

"Mr Smurthwaite! Mr Smurthwaite!" we kept calling.

We crept about. Things were so lovely, all the big thick carpets and the velvet hangings, I could have gazed for hours. Then all of a sudden we heard a funny noise. '*Gloog-gloog-gloog*!'

When I say funny, I mean weird. Horrible, really. It sounded like a drain. Yet it sounded like a person, too.

"Come on, Henry!" I seized his arm. I wanted to run away. But Henry didn't. He got bold, all of a sudden.

He tiptoed off in the direction of the noise, and pushed open a door. Then he called out in fright!

"Quick, Annie, come here at once!"

I crept over. I was shivering already,

wondering what I would see. But I never
thought of seeing anything like I did.

There in that big room was a carpet. It was
rolled up and fastened with cord. Right in the
middle, like the jam in a doughnut, was the
head of a man. The man who was making the
noises.

"It's *you*, Mr Smurthwaite!" cried Henry.
"Whatever are you doing in there?"

4 Annie holds on bravely

"Gloog-gloog," gasped Mr Smurthwaite. His
eyes went everywhere. His round face was
bright scarlet. What was he trying to say? He
seemed to be telling us to find a knife – but
where? We looked about. We found the
kitchen, and looked in different drawers.

I nudged Henry. "Perhaps we should ring up
the police?" I suggested.

"I'll ask him." He knelt down by Mr
Smurthwaite's face. But the voice said the
telephone was cut. Again the voice said, "Get a
knife, get a knife!"

I went out into a big hall where a wide
staircase was, and I heard a voice from the top
of the house. Other people! What a relief!

I started off up the stairs, and when I got to the top, I heard it again.

It was a man's voice – where had I heard it before?

"WELL DONE!" It croaked again and again, "WELL DONE!"

I opened the door, and soon wished I hadn't. A rough-looking man was in the room, kneeling on the floor, and guess what he was doing! Yes, playing with NIPPY NUMBERS. Here was my toy all right, or rather Mr Trencham's, and at once something told me it had fallen into the hands of a crook.

The man saw me and gave a shout, but I
didn't have time to hear what he said. It
sounded like "Get out, you!" But he needn't
have bothered. The wide stairs were not easy
to hurry down, but I slithered down them as if
lions were chasing me. I was so upset, I would
have been thankful to join Mr Smurthwaite
inside his carpet, if needs be.

By now Henry had got hold of a knife. He
was hacking away at the thick cord round the
carpet. Poor Mr Smurthwaite, his eyes were
nearly popping out of his head.

"Quick, boy, quick!" he gasped.

Henry did his best. It wasn't easy. The knife
was blunt, and the cord was hard. But he sawed

away as best he could. At last one bit gave way,
then another. When all the strings were cut,
Henry and I pushed with all our might against
the carpet. Slowly it went over – and over –
and over –

It took all our strength, but at last it was
done. The carpet was flat. Mr Smurthwaite lay
flat, too, for a moment, like a fish on land. Then
he rose up slowly, and shook himself, and
stretched out his arms and legs.

He was in a dreadful rage. His face was so red
it might have been on fire. "Can thee believe
it, can thee believe it," he kept shouting. If we

two hadn't been young children, I expect he would have given way to bad language.

I'd never seen Mr Smurthwaite before, but I quite liked the look of him. Although he was in such a temper, I thought his face was kind. He was a short, fat man, and I could understand his voice quite well. I have an auntie from the north who talks like he does. He shook both

our hands, then said there was no time to lose, so would Henry please go and call the police from a public call box?

After Henry had gone, Mr Smurthwaite drank some water and tossed some over his face. He began to calm down and said he was very glad to see Henry and me, we had arrived in the nick of time. "Shall I tell thee what's been happening, little Duchess?"

"Oh yes," I said, "please do!"

Mr Smurthwaite said he'd been out in the kitchen boiling a kettle when hands had come from behind and seized him. Next thing, he was being carried about by three men. They laid him out on a carpet, and rolled him up like a sausage.

I almost wanted to laugh, but didn't dare, for at the very word 'sausage' Mr Smurthwaite turned quite red again, and began to dance about excitedly. "They won't get away with it, thee'll see! And I'll tell thee why not. They can't get their get-away car to go. So now one of 'em's rooshed off to fetch a spanner."

"And when he – rooshes back?" I said, giving Mr Smurthwaite's word a try. After all, you spell *rush* like *bush* so why not pronounce it the same?

"When he *rooshes* back," said Mr Smurthwaite, grinning, "he'll have a big surprise, Duchess. There'll be me waiting, and thee, and little Henry, and we hope some big policemen."

"Er –" I began, "I expect you wonder why Henry and I came here. You see, we were looking for this – er – game, Mr Smurthwaite. The one you bought from Henry's grandmother at the Village Hall. It's called NIPPY NUMBERS. There are these questions, and if you get them right, a voice says 'WELL DONE!'"

"Well done?" repeated Mr Smurthwaite, echoing my croaky cry absent-mindedly. I could see he wasn't listening properly. Suddenly he ran to the window and looked out. An idea

seemed to have struck him. "I've got it!" he announced. "I'm going out there, and I'm going to let down their tyres, you see, Duchess!"

"Oh good, I'll come with you." I didn't at all fancy being left in Benson House all on my own. I started explaining to Mr Smurthwaite that there was a strange man upstairs, but he didn't hear. With a wave of his hand, he told me to stay where I was. I would be quite safe, and the police would be here any minute.

Off he pelted. There I stood. When I say there, please remember the place! Just by the carpet. *The* carpet. The magic carpet, if you like; I've heard stories of such a thing. But the carpet in the stories flew through the air. *This* carpet lay quietly on the floor. Yet not long ago it had been used to parcel up poor Mr Smurthwaite! And might next, for all I knew, be used to parcel up poor Annie Ironside!

As usual, my mind flew to my big sister, Carole. It always does, in times of stress and strain.

I mentioned that song she keeps singing:
'No regrets, no regrets,

I'm never sorry,
Never worry,
Yah, yah, keep yer moans
Flesh is flesh and bones is bones –'
and again I'd add, that's exactly the way Carole
seems to think herself. People never upset her.
She doesn't let them. Well, it does happen that
she gets annoyed with me sometimes. I mean,
she calls me all sorts of names, and goes red in
the face, and complains about me to our mum.
But really that is because she daren't do what
she'd like to do, which is to give me a punch
on the nose.

What I mean is, she never gets nervous. If
she'd been in my place now, her throat
wouldn't have been going THUD, THUD, THUD
like mine was. She would have had everybody
running round looking after her, making sure
she was all right.

Isn't it funny how you can dream things,
even while you are awake? I mean, pictures can
come into your head, they can just flash through
it in just a second. Even at this moment when
I was so frightened and so worked-up, standing

112

all alone in this great room in Benson House,
I could just see Carole strutting past, tossing
her head as if to say, "Pah – try rolling *me* up
in a carpet, men!" I wished I was brave like
her. If I was, I'd dash upstairs and say to that –
(I didn't want to think about him really) –
that, er, peculiar person:

"Give me back that toy immediately!"

Suddenly, I heard a door bang upstairs. A
real one! Next, feet on the stairs. I dropped
down behind a sofa. The feet drew near. I
crouched trembling in my hiding-place. The
rest of the world seemed to stop. I don't know
how long all this took. Maybe it wasn't very
long. But it felt like for ever.

Then the front door rattled, opened, and banged shut. A moment later, I heard a car drive away.

Back rushed Mr Smurthwaite. I hadn't realised it was possible for him to get into an even worse temper.

It seemed the car I had heard drive away was his! Yes, he'd opened the door of his pick-up to take out some tools, and hadn't shut it properly, and the thief, seeing it open, had jumped in and driven off.

"Under my very eyes! There are limits to what a man can take!"

Poor Mr Smurthwaite. He was just launching into shouts of, "I'll get those villains yet," when Henry Renny appeared, with two very calm-looking policemen. You would have thought he was in charge of them, he looked so proud.

"So what is the problem here?" asked the largest.

"Problem!" After dancing about a bit, Mr Smurthwaite calmed down. He said that three villains had broken into the house, overpowered

him, and tied him up in a carpet. He thought
they had gathered some stolen goods together,
but couldn't get them away, because their car
had broken down.

"Surely Mr Peggs's car couldn't break
down?" Henry objected. "It never did before."

"It may have run out of petrol," suggested
one of the policemen. As he spoke, two more
policemen arrived. You'll never guess who they
had with them.

Mr Peggs!

All eight of us stood staring at one another. The air was simply full of astonishment. That's the only way to describe it. Then Henry shouted out, ''We got it, Mr Peggs, we got it, *we got your car!*''

Mr Peggs smiled grimly, but I could tell he was truly thankful.

5 Sorting out the treasure

Mr Peggs was very angry to discover that his car had been painted red. Nor did he thank Mr Smurthwaite for letting down his tyres.

"A little service I could have done without!" he said, smiling grimly again. He cheered up a little when he heard that poor Mr Smurthwaite's pick-up had been stolen, too.

"The thieves were too nippy for you, then!" He had a good laugh.

At the word 'nippy' my mind flew to the famous toy. I tried mentioning it to Mr Smurthwaite again, but he only seemed interested in his pick-up.

"Now, sir," the biggest policeman said to him, "will you take us round the premises?"

117

I don't know if they needed Henry and me,
but we stuck to them like leeches. "I know
where it is," I whispered to Henry. He didn't
seem interested in NIPPY NUMBERS either, but
nothing was going to stop him from marching
about with a set of policemen. He kept looking
up at them and beaming. You'd have thought
nobody knew how to cope with crime better
than Henry Renny.

What a beautiful house! How I wished my
friend Cynthia had been there, too! She loves
pretty places. But I was still too worked up
about Mr Trencham's toy to gaze admiringly at
each fine room we entered. All the same, I did
notice one where the backward boy must play
sometimes. There were big charts over the walls,
showing pictures with numbers against them –
six pies, *five* hens; there was even one which
showed ten cakes; and then, after a fat child
ate six, *four* cakes! It showed the child eating
them.

Jolly helpful, I thought, I must tell Mr
Trencham about those.

"Hey, little girl, is that what thee's been
looking for?" asked Mr Smurthwaite, jogging
my elbow.

He pointed to a table. We had by this time
come to the very room where the crafty-looking
man had been, and there on the table, lid off
but in one piece, sat NIPPY NUMBERS.

Mr Peggs leaned forward and fixed his glassy
gaze on Mr Trencham's famous toy. "What is
that?"

"Summat these two were seeking," said Mr Smurthwaite, smiling kindly, "these two little people here."

"I do believe it is something from our school!" Mr Peggs inspected the lid. "The rogues who stole my car must have snatched it up. See," he pointed at the floor, which was strewn with coke tins and fag-ends, "they have been up here, with their rubbish, and had the cheek to include school apparatus in their booty! Can you believe it?" he asked, swinging round to the four policemen.

While they were shaking their heads, he told me to take NIPPY NUMBERS back to school with me. I didn't bother to tell him about Mr Smurthwaite buying it as jumble. Mr Peggs is not the sort of person who you tell things like that.

The great thing was: NIPPY NUMBERS was in my arms. The precious game was safe and sound at last. It was heavier than I remembered, but I wasn't letting go of it in a million years.

"NIPPY NUMBERS," exclaimed Mr Smurthwaite with a smile, "they have some great ideas at schools, nowadays, don't they?"

The burglary up at Benson House made everybody in Pennymarsh very excited. They talked about it all the time. Some said the thieves had got away with a big haul. Others said they'd taken nothing. Several were sure they'd seen odd-looking people roaming round Pennymarsh lately. Both Barry and his brother were sure they'd noticed two men with long hair swinging bicycle chains round their shoulders. Cynthia thought she'd heard odd

noises several nights ago, and somebody singing
softly under her window. All agreed that the
thieves' get-away car, (now safely back with its
owner and put away under its plastic dome),
was to have been Mr Peggs's Rover.

Nobody had a good word to say for poor
Mr Smurthwaite. If I heard him called fishy
once, I heard him called it six times. Soon I had
to stop boasting about Henry and me and the
carpet, because, firstly, nobody believed me,
and, secondly, they started thinking I was
fishy, too.

As for NIPPY NUMBERS, put safely away in a
cupboard, my mum couldn't get it out of her
head. "But why did Mr Trencham lend it to
you, Annie? He ought not to have entrusted it
to a little girl. Look at the trouble it's caused!
Trust you to go and get yourself involved with
a set of criminals!"

"Oh Mum, you've got it all wrong. Mr
Trencham was trying to be helpful. Besides, he
could trust me. Look at all I went through on
his account! Think how Henry and I rescued
Mr Smurthwaite!"

"I'd rather not, Annie. If anybody lends you anything again, will you be sure to tell me?"

"Oh, I'm not borrowing any more things, thanks, Mum."

My mother and Carole sat at home staring at me. I do believe in a way they envied me

having such adventures. They wanted to hear all about Benson House, which they'd never been inside in their lives. They kept asking me about dull things I'd never noticed; like, how many bathrooms were there? What was the kitchen like? Was the cooker gas or electric?

"Did I tell you what one of the policemen said, Mum?" I asked, trying to steer talk round to something more interesting. "He said we were two brave children, full of . . . of . . . something that sounded like sauce: what's the word?"

"Tomato sauce?" suggested Carole.

"No! Re – re –"

"Resourcefulness?" said my mother.

"That's it! He said we were full of resourcefulness. He said that if he had his way, we would both get a medal."

"Did he now? The Victoria Cross, perhaps?"

The two started laughing. You might have thought they would have been proud of me, going through such a lot, for the sake of NIPPY NUMBERS, but not at all.

124

"Can't you see, Mum, that I come out of this jolly well?"

"If you say so, Annie," she replied with a sigh.

Isn't it funny how your own family never give you credit?

Wednesday came at last. Mr Trencham stood in the school doorway, running his hand through his thin hair and blinking. I smiled at him from our table. When he came and sat down, I said with a sigh of relief, "All's well, Mr Trencham! I've brought back what you lent me."

"What did I lend you, Annie?"

"You know! NIPPY NUMBERS."

He stared at me. I stared back. Then I realised – why, he'd forgotten all about it!

"You must remember, Mr Trencham!" It couldn't be true. It was.

Gradually, light dawned. "NIPPY NUMBERS!" he exclaimed. "What a dreadful name. Yes, of course I remember. Ever since some chap brought it into the office, it's been nothing but a nuisance to me."

125

"Oh, and to *me*," I said, "you'd never *believe* what a nuisance, Mr Trencham!"

"Did it teach you anything?"

"Well –" I hesitated. "Yes and no, really." I pointed to it. "I put it in a plastic bag," I said, "so it didn't get scratched or dirty."

"I think I'll put it in my car straightaway," said Mr Trencham, "before I go and forget about it."

As he hurried off, old Miss Tubb walked in. I suddenly remembered the bit she'd read out of her Bible. About moth and rust attacking people's treasures and thieves breaking in.

Perhaps she'd read it to Mr Trencham, when he came back.